PRAISE FOR ÁGOTA KRIST

"Startling brutality and ferocit
—Eimear McBride, *The Believe*

"The sublime refinement of her craft comes close to knocking the breath out of our bodies." —Helen Oyeyemi

"Kristóf will reassemble a shattered world on her own rigorous terms, and watch us wince and shudder in the process." —*Times Literary Supplement*

"Chillingly unsentimental." —*Sunday Times*

"When I first heard someone talk about Ágota Kristóf, I thought it was an east European mispronunciation of Agatha Christie; but I soon discovered not only that Ágota is not Agatha, but that Ágota's horror is much more terrifying than Agatha's." —Slavoj Žižek, *The Guardian*

"Mischievous and mournful: moves at a velocity that puts one in mind of Italo Calvino." —*Publishers Weekly*

"Many of her stark vignettes, reported in unflinching detail, have a cool, disturbing power—part documentary-like, part surreal— that is fierce and distinctive." —*Kirkus Reviews*

"Lingers in the imagination long after you've turned the last page." —*The Washington Post Book World*

"Ágota Kristóf should perhaps be seen as our transnational bard." —Gabriel Josipovici

# I DON'T CARE

ALSO BY ÁGOTA KRISTÓF

*The Illiterate*

Trilogy: *The Notebook, The Proof, The Third Lie*

ÁGOTA KRISTÓF

# *I Don't Care*

*translated from the French by* Chris Andrews

A NEW DIRECTIONS
PAPERBOOK ORIGINAL

Originally published in French as *C'est égal* by Éditions de Seuil in 2004.
Published by arrangement with Éditions de Seuil.

Manufactured in the United States of America
First published as New Directions Paperbook 1610 in 2024

*Library of Congress Cataloging-in-Publication Data*
Names: Kristof, Agota, author. | Andrews, Chris, 1962– translator.
Title: I don't care / Ágota Kristóf ;
translated from the French by Chris Andrews.
Other titles: C'est égal. English | I do not care
Description: New York : New Directions Publishing Corporation, 2024.
Identifiers: LCCN 2024032042 | ISBN 9780811235167 (paperback) |
ISBN 9780811235174 (ebook)
Subjects: LCGFT: Short stories.
Classification: LCC PQ2671.R55 C4713 2024 | DDC 843/.914—dc23/eng/20240722
LC record available at https://lccn.loc.gov/2024032042

10 9 8 7 6 5 4 3 2 1

New Directions Books are published for James Laughlin
by New Directions Publishing Corporation
80 Eighth Avenue, New York 10011

# *Contents*

# I DON'T CARE

## *I Don't Care*

Above, below, blue heads, thistles.
Somebody singing something.
I don't care: it's not even pretty. The song is sad, and old, so old.
—And tomorrow? You get up, where do you go?
—Nowhere. Or, I don't know, maybe I will go somewhere.
I don't care, anyway, nowhere feels right.
But it's hard to sleep, with the bells that clang, and the clocks.

—Spread out your handkerchief, sir. I would like to kneel down.
—Be my guest.
There were two of them in the tram. One to ring the bell, one to punch the tickets.
No one left to get off at the terminus.
But that is where all the trams come to a halt.
No one there to get on either.
They don't care.
They kneel down, exchange a few words.
—Would you like to exchange a few words with me?

—I thought you wanted to pray.

—I'm done.

—In that case, then, we can head back. I'll call you tomorrow.

—What's new?

—How are your children?

—Thanks for asking. Only two of them are sick, for the moment. The older ones go into stores, to warm up. How about you?

—Nothing special. Our dog is housebroken now. We bought some furniture on credit. From time to time, it snows.

## *I Have Given Up Eating*

It's too late now. I have given up eating. I refuse bread and tantrums. I also refuse the maternal breast on offer to all newcomers in the dairies of grief.

As soon as I learned how to live, I was fed corn and beans.

Stealing our few potatoes from the infinite fields of my native land, I built a shrine to all the untasted delicacies.

Now I have a white tablecloth, crystal and silverware, but the salmon and the saddle of venison came too late.

I have given up eating.

With a smile, I raise my glass filled with a rare wine to toast my dinner guests. I set my glass down empty; my fine white fingers caress the tablecloth's embroidered flowers.

I remember . . .

And I laugh as I watch my guests avidly tucking into the jugged hare, which I bagged myself in the cramped fields of their native land.

And which, in fact, is just their favorite pet cat.

## *The Canal*

The man was watching his life desert him.

A few yards away, his car was still burning.

The ground was red and white—blood and snow, menses and sperm—and beyond: indigo mountains hung with a necklace of lights.

The man was thinking:

"They switch them on too soon. It's not dark yet. Stars—I don't know their names. I never have."

Nausea, vertigo. The man falls asleep again, and dreams the same dream, the same nightmare, always the same.

He walks the streets of the city of his birth, trying to find his son. His son who is waiting in one of the houses, the house where the man once waited for his own father.

The problem is, he's lost; nothing looks familiar any more. Impossible to find his street, his house.

"They've changed everything… everything."

He comes to the main square. The houses all around him shine, yes, houses made of yellow metal and glass, soaring up to the clouds.

"What have they done? It's monstrous."

Then he understands.

They have found gold. The gold the old people used to talk about, the gold in the rocks, in the legends. They have found it and built a city out of gold, one of a kind, a nightmare city.

He leaves the square, and finds himself in a broad, old street, lined with wooden houses and dilapidated barns. The ground is dusty and pleasant to walk on barefoot.

"This is my street. I have found it. I'm not lost any more. Nothing's changed here."

And yet there's a strange tension in the air.

The man turns and sees the puma at the other end of the street.

A splendid animal, beige and golden; its silky fur shines in the burning sun.

Everything burns. The houses and the barns burst into flames, but he must keep walking between the two walls of fire because the puma has started walking too, following him at a distance with a majestically slow tread.

"Where to hide? There's no way out. The flames or the fangs. Maybe at the end of the street? This street must end somewhere. The infinite does not exist. All streets have to come to an end; they lead to a square, or another street. Help!"

He has cried out. The puma is close now, just behind him. The man doesn't dare turn around but can't keep walking; his feet have taken root. With unspeakable dread he waits for the animal to leap onto his back at last, tear him open from shoulder to thigh, and maul his head.

But the puma overtakes him, continuing imperturbably on its way, and lies down at the feet of a child who has appeared out of nowhere and is now stroking the animal's head.

The child looks at the man, who is paralyzed with fear.

—He's not vicious; he's mine. You shouldn't be afraid of him; he doesn't eat meat, only souls.

The flames have died away. The blaze has gone out. The whole street has been reduced to soft, cool ash.

A smile lights up the man's features.

—Perhaps you are my son? Were you waiting for me?

—I wasn't waiting for anyone, but yes, you're my father. Follow me.

The child leads him to the edge of the city, where a river flows, its surface a shimmering yellow under powerful floodlights. Dark silhouettes drift by on the current, face up, eyes turned to the starry sky.

The man snickers.

—Dreamboats? Old crocks, more like it. I recognize them: it's my father and mother in the waters of the river of eternal youth.

Golden, still as a sculpture, the puma is stretched out against the facade of an enormous building.

—No, says the puma, you're too stupid. Don't laugh. This isn't the river of eternal youth; these are the waters of the city's drains, carrying the waste away. The dead and everything people want to get rid of: guilt, mistakes, desertions, betrayals, crimes, murders.

—Have there been murders?

—Yes. All that is carried away by the clear water of redemption. But the dead return, the sea won't take them. It washes them into another canal, which brings them back here. Then they drift around the city, like the souls of olden times.

—They look happy, though.

—Their faces are set in eternally polite expressions. But who can tell what they're feeling?

—You, probably.

—I can see only the outside. I observe.

—And what do you observe?

—That every outside surrounded by another outside becomes an inside, just as surely as an inside that lets an inside in becomes an outside.

—I don't understand.

—It doesn't matter. You will die, you will fall into the canal and drift around the city.

—No. If I die, I'm going to fly to the stars.

—Birds fall too when they die, and anyway, you don't even have wings.

—And my son?

—He's right there, behind you. He's the one who will help you.

The child raises his delicate hand to touch the man's back, and the man falls without a cry. He lets the water of the canal carry him away, his eyes fixed on the stars he can no longer see.

The child walks off, shrugging his shoulders.

The puma sighs:

—That's how it is, from generation to generation.

He rests his big head on his front paws, and the whole building comes tumbling down.

## *The Invitation*

On Friday evening, the husband comes back from the office in a cheerful mood.

—Tomorrow's your birthday, darling. Let's have a party; we'll invite some friends. I'll give you your little present at the end of the month; I'm a bit short right now. What would you like? A nice wristwatch?

—I already have a watch, darling. I'm very happy with it.

—A dress then. A little designer-type outfit?

—Designer-*type*! I need trousers and a pair of sandals, that's all.

—Up to you. I'll give you the money and you can choose what you like. But not until the end of the month. The party, though, we can do that tomorrow, with a bunch of friends.

—You know, said his wife, these parties with a bunch of friends, they're kind of tiring for me. I'd prefer to have dinner at a good restaurant.

—Restaurants are a rip-off, and you can't be sure it'll be good. I'd rather give you a good dinner at home. I'll take care of everything: the shopping, the menu, the invitations. You can go to the hairdresser and get dolled up, and everything will be ready on time. All you'll have to do is sit down at the table. I'll even serve it; that'll be fun to do, for once.

So Mr. Husband sets about organizing the party. He's in his element. He has Saturday afternoon off. He goes shopping. He comes back around five, loaded up and beaming.

—It's going to be great, he says to his wife. You might want to set the table, that'd save us some time.

With her hair freshly done, wearing a little black dress from twenty years ago, she sets the table and succeeds in decorating it very prettily.

Her husband appears:

—You should have put out the champagne flutes. I'll fix it. While I'm doing that, light the fire, will you; I'm going to grill the chops over it—so good! Then if you could come and peel the potatoes and make the salad dressing. Yuck, the lettuces are full of little creepy-crawlies, tiny slugs. Disgusting! Do you think you could wash them? You know how to do it.

And later, from his post by the fire:

—That should give us enough coals. Could you bring me a glass of gin with ... Hang on, do we have lemons for the gin? No, I didn't buy any. I thought we had some. You could at least have thought about the aperitifs; I can't do everything. I think Chez Marco's still open. Get some almonds and hazelnuts, too. And olives!

Fifteen minutes later.

—I knew it would be open. Haven't you put the potatoes on yet? I have to keep an eye on the chops. Oh,

I nearly forgot: I bought shrimp for the entrée. Whip up a little sauce with cream and ketchup. There's no ketchup? There's never anything in this place! Nip up and borrow some from So-and-So.

Mrs. Wife goes upstairs to ask So-and-So for some ketchup. So-and-So is happy to lend her his bottle of ketchup, but as a bonus, insists on relating the woes of the day, and of his life in general.

Downstairs the doorbell rings; the guests arrive. Mrs. Wife must go back down.

The friends are sitting around the fire.

The husband cries out:

—What's with those aperitifs, Madeleine?

The chops are done, finally. A bit overdone. But there's a good ambience. Plenty of drinking. And laughter. Madeleine's age is mentioned a little too often, but it's her birthday, after all. The friends also sing the praises of the man who prepared and organized everything.

—What a dream husband.

—Lucky you. And after fifteen years of marriage.

—Got to hand it to you, old buddy!

Around three in the morning, suddenly, it all goes quiet.

The friends have left; the husband is snoring on the couch in the living room, exhausted, poor thing.

Madeleine empties the ashtrays, collects the empty bottles, the dirty glasses, the pieces of broken glass; she clears the table.

Before starting to wash up, she goes to the bathroom and takes a long look at herself in the mirror.

## *A Northbound Train*

A sculpture in a park, near an abandoned railway station.

It represents a man and a dog.

The dog is standing, the man is on his knees, with his arms around the dog's neck and his head slightly tilted.

The dog's eyes look out over the plain that stretches off endlessly to the left of the station; the man's eyes stare fixedly straight ahead, over the dog's back, at the rails overgrown with weeds, on which no train has run for a long time. The village that was once served by the derelict station has been abandoned. A few city dwellers partial to nature and solitude still spend the summer months here, but they all have cars.

There is also the old man who wanders around the park and claims that he sculpted the dog and that, one day when hugging it—since he loved the animal dearly—he was turned to stone.

When asked how it is that he is still there, nevertheless, alive, in the flesh, he answers simply that he is waiting for the next train north.

No one has the heart to tell him that there are no

more northbound trains, or trains bound anywhere. People offer him a lift in their cars, but he shakes his head.

—No, not by car. They're waiting for me at the station.

People offer to take him to the station, to any station in the north.

Again, he shakes his head.

—No thank you. I have to take the train. I have sent letters. To my mother. To my wife as well. I said that I would be arriving on the 8 p.m. train. My wife is waiting for me at the station with the children. My mother is waiting for me too. Since my father died she has been waiting for me to come back so she can bury him. I promised her I would come for his funeral. I'm also hoping to see my wife and children, although I . . . abandoned them. Yes, abandoned. In order to become a great artist. I painted, I sculpted. Now I want to go home.

—But all that, the letters to your mother and your wife, your father's funeral, when was all that?

—All that was . . . when I poisoned my dog, because he wouldn't let me leave. He pulled at my coat, my trousers. He howled when I tried to board the train. So I poisoned him, and buried him under the sculpture.

—The sculpture was already here?

—No, I sculpted it the next day. I sculpted my dog here, on his grave. And when the northbound train arrived, I hugged him one last time and turned to stone, my arms around his neck. Even dead, he wouldn't let me leave.

—But here you are, waiting for a train.

The old man laughs:

—I'm not as crazy as you think. I know very well I don't exist; I'm a mass of stone, clinging to the back of my dog. And I know that the trains no longer run on this line. I also know that my father was buried a long time ago, and that my mother, who's dead too, isn't waiting for me at any station. No one is waiting for me. My wife remarried and my children are grown up. I am old, sir, very old, even older than you think. I am a statue; I'll never leave. By now all this is just a game between my dog and me, a game we've played for years, a game he won the moment I set eyes on him.

## *The Axe*

"Come in, Doctor. Yes, it's here. Yes, I'm the one who called you. My husband has had an accident. Yes, I think it's a serious accident. In fact, very serious. Upstairs. He's in our bedroom. This way. Sorry, the bed's not made. I panicked a bit, you know, when I saw all the blood. I don't know how I'm going to face cleaning it up. I think I'll just go live somewhere else.

"Here's the room, come in. There he is, beside the bed, on the rug. There's an axe stuck in his head. Do you want to examine him? Go on, examine him. A really stupid accident, isn't it? He fell out of bed, onto that axe, in his sleep.

"Yes, the axe is ours. Normally it's in the living room, beside the fireplace; we use it to chop kindling.

"Why was it beside the bed? I've got no idea. He must have propped it against the bedside table. Maybe he was worried about burglars. We're pretty isolated out here.

"He's dead, is he? That's what I thought, right away. But I said to myself: Better get a doctor to check.

"You want to make a call? Ah yes, the ambulance. No? The police? Why the police? It's an accident. He just fell out of bed, onto an axe. It is unusual, yes. But stupid things like that happen all the time.

"Oh, maybe you're thinking I put the axe beside the bed so he'd fall on it? But how could I know he was going to fall out of bed?

"Maybe you even think I pushed him, and then went peacefully to sleep, alone at last in our big bed, without the sound of his snoring, and the smell of him!

"Come on, Doctor, surely you can't be imagining something like that ...

"I did sleep well, it's true. I haven't slept so well for years. I didn't wake up until eight. I looked out the window. It was windy. Puffy gray and white clouds were playing in the sky, hiding the sun. I was happy, and I thought: You can never tell with clouds. Maybe they would scatter—they were blowing so fast—maybe they would gather and settle on our shoulders as rain. I didn't care. I love rain. Besides, this morning everything seemed wonderful. I felt relieved, after so long, freed of a burden ...

"And that's when I turned around and saw the accident, and I called you right away.

"You want to make a call too. There's the phone. You're calling the ambulance. To have the body taken away, is that it?

"What do you mean, it's for me? I don't understand. I'm not hurt. There's nothing wrong with me; I feel fine. The blood on my nightie, that's just a bit of my husband's blood that spattered when ... "

## *At Home*

Will it be in this life or another?

I will go home.

Outside, the trees will howl, but they won't scare me, nor will the red clouds, or the lights of the city.

I will go home, to a home I never had, or so long ago I can't remember it, because it was never mine, not really.

Tomorrow, at last, I will have my real home, in a poor neighborhood in a big city. A poor neighborhood, because how can you get rich when you start with nothing, and come from elsewhere, from nowhere, without any desire to get rich?

A big city, because in the small ones there are just a few houses for the disinherited; only big cities have street after dark street, endlessly, where people like myself lie low.

I will walk through those streets toward my house.

I will walk through those wind-lashed, moonlit streets.

Fat women, getting some fresh air, will watch me pass without saying a word. I will greet everyone, brimming with happiness. Nearly naked children will bump into my legs. I will scoop them up, remembering my own, who will be grown by then, rich and happy, somewhere. I will caress those children, whoever they belong to, and offer them shiny, rare objects. I will pick up the drunken man fallen in the gutter, and comfort the woman who runs howling in the night; I will listen to her suffering, calm her.

When I get home I will be tired. I will lie down on the bed, any bed, and the curtains will float like clouds.

Time will pass like this.

And inside my eyelids, images will pass, the images of the bad dream that was my life.

But they will no longer hurt me.

I will be at home, alone, old, and happy.

## *Death of a Worker*

The unfinished syllable hung without meaning between the window and the vase of flowers.

The unfinished gesture of your weakened fingers, drawing half a capital *N* on the sheets.

—No!

You thought if you only kept your eyes open, death would not be able to touch you. You held them wide open as long as you possibly could, but night came and took you in its arms.

Just yesterday you were thinking of your car and how you didn't finish washing it that Saturday, so long ago already, when the pain first punched you in the stomach.

—Cancer, said the doctor, and your hospital bed's cleanness filled you with horror.

As the days, the weeks, the months went by, even your hands turned white. Gone, the stubborn oil stains; nails no longer broken but intact and pink, like a civil servant's.

In the evenings, you wept silently, without sobs or blubbering, just tears running gently onto the pillow, without a sound, in the ward where the green glow of the night-lights bathed the faces of your sick neighbors, sinking trenches in their cheeks and under their eyes.

No, you were not alone.

There were six or seven of you waiting to die from one day to the next.

As at the factory. You weren't alone there either; there were twenty of you, or fifty, performing the same operation from one day to the next.

It wasn't only watches your factory manufactured; it manufactured corpses too.

And in the hospital as at the factory, you had nothing to say to each other.

You thought the others were asleep, or already dead.

The others thought you were asleep, or already dead.

None of them spoke, nor did you.

You no longer wanted to speak; you only wanted to remember something, something, but you didn't know what.

There was nothing to remember.

Your memories, your youth, your strength, your life: the factory had taken them. All it had left you was weariness, the mortal weariness of forty years of work.

## *The Writer*

I have retired to write my masterpiece.

I am a great writer. No one knows it yet, because I haven't yet written anything. But when I write my book, my novel . . .

That's why I retired from my job as a civil servant and from . . . what else? That's all, really. As for friends, I never had any, let alone girlfriends. Still, I have retired from the world to write a great novel.

The problem is, I don't know what the subject of my novel will be. So much has already been written about anything and everything.

I sense, I feel that I am a great writer, but no subject seems good enough, big enough, interesting enough for my talent.

So I'm waiting. And obviously, while I wait, I suffer from loneliness, and sometimes hunger, but it is by this suffering that I hope to reach the spiritual state that will allow me to discover a subject worthy of my talent.

Unfortunately, the subject keeps delaying its appearance, and my solitude is growing heavier and harder to bear. Silence surrounds me, the void is encroaching from all directions, and it's not as if I have a lot of space here.

Solitude, silence, and the void—that horrible trio—blow my roof open, they fly up to the stars, reach away to infinity, and I can't tell any more if it's raining or snowing, if it's the foehn or the monsoon.

And I cry out:

—I will write everything, everything that can be written.

And a voice answers me, ironically, but at least there is a voice:

—All right, son. Everything, but that's all, OK?

## *The Child*

They sit there, at a table on a café terrace. They watch the people passing by. People pass, as usual, as anyone might, or must, they pass. People like taking turns to pass by.

Me, I dawdle and drag along after them. I rage, I stop, I spit, I cry, then I sit on the curb and stick my tongue out at all the people passing by.

—You're rude, say the passersby.

—Yes, we're ashamed of you, say my parents.

I'm ashamed of them too. They didn't buy me the rifle, the nice rifle I wanted. They said:

—It's not a nice toy.

But I saw my father going off to do his military service. He had a rifle, a real one, for killing. And when I saw nice rifles for children, Indian rifles, for hunting, for playing, they said they were very nasty toys, and they bought me a spinning top!

Here I am, sitting on the curb. I get up, I rage, I cry, I spit, I shout:

—You're rude, I'm ashamed of you: you tell lies, you pretend to be kind! When I grow up, I'm going to kill you!

## *The House*

He was ten years old. He was sitting on the sidewalk, watching as furniture and boxes were loaded onto a truck.

—What are they doing? he asked another boy from the street who had come to sit down beside him.

—Moving out, of course! said the other boy. I'd like to be a mover. It's a great job. You have to be strong.

—You mean they're going to live in another house?

—Obviously, if they're moving.

—Poor things. Has something bad happened to them?

—What do you mean bad? It's the opposite. They'll be going to a house that's bigger and prettier. If I it were me, I'd be happy.

He went home, sat on the grass in the garden, and cried.

—You can't do that, leave one house for another; it's terrible, like if somebody got killed.

By the age of fifteen, he was living in another city. They moved in winter. Through the window of the train, he watched his childhood receding into the distance. Then, with a smile, he said to his mother:

—I hope you'll like it there.

But one day, a Sunday at the beginning of June, he revisited the old house.

The neighbor, an invalid who had always liked that polite, quiet little boy, was very happy to see him again.

—Sit down, and tell me what you've been up to in the big city.

—Nothing has changed here, replied the boy, looking around the single room. Do you mind if I go out into the garden?

With one step, he was over the hedge and back home. The air was laden with the scent of overripe strawberries, spoiling in the sun.

He stepped forward and saw the house.

It was standing there, still and empty.

—You look tired, he said to it, but you must be able to tell I'm back.

From then on he visited the house each week, looked at it, and spoke to it.

—Are you suffering as much as I am? he asked one afternoon when the October rain was beating pitilessly against the gray walls of the house, and the windows were rattling in the wind.

—Don't cry, he shouted, sobbing. I promise I'll come back and stay forever.

A man leaned out of a window, looking crossly into the garden.

—There's someone in there, whispered the boy, shattered by grief. You've found someone else. You don't love me any more. I hate that man!

The window banged shut, and the train departed, flying away over the dead fields.

Soon an ocean came between them, and time.

The boy was no longer a boy but a man.

Time, the ocean, the big city lights, and the houses that reach up to the clouds whispered to him in the night:

—You see, you see how far away you are, how far from me.

The faces, the crowd of faces, those uniform faces, the noise, the senseless din, so monotone it resembles silence, and the clocks, the bells, the alarms, the telephones, the padded doors, the murmuring elevators, the laughter, the mad, unbearable music.

Above all that, a resigned, almost ridiculous voice, a distant, sad, old voice:

—You see how far from me you are. You have abandoned me; you have forgotten me.

The little boy was now a rich man. So he decided to reconstruct his house, his first house. He had several already. One beside the sea, another in a fancy neighborhood, a chalet in the mountains. But he wanted to possess the first, the only one.

He consulted an architect and gave him a muddled description of his childhood home.

The architect smiled. He was constantly called upon to realize plans unrelated to reality:

—I need precise numbers, measurements. Without measurements I can't do anything.

—Yes, I understand. I'll write to them; I'll get it

measured. The important thing is the veranda, and the vine climbing the walls. And we mustn't forget the dust on the leaves and the bunches of grapes.

When the house was built, he nodded:

—Yes, it's exactly the same.

He smiled, but his eyes were empty.

A few days later he left without a word to anyone.

He went from one place, one city to another, taking planes, boats, trains.

Always somewhere new, where nothing resembled the house. The cold lights of the big cities, beautiful and different: impossible even to dream of loving them.

—I had a copy made. Ridiculous. As if you could copy what you once knew.

A luxury hotel, no resemblance. A carpet on the steps, a carpet in the hall.

—A letter for you, sir.

He opens the letter in the elevator.

"Why did you leave?"

A shock.

But houses don't write letters. It's just his wife.

"Why did you leave?"

Yes, why?

The letter lies on the table. Tomorrow, the trains will roll away on rails screeching with fatigue.

The rails are so fatigued the train has to stop in the middle of nowhere. Technical hitch.

A man steps out of the first-class sleeping car. No one pays him any attention. He climbs down the embankment and finds himself in a dead, muddy field. The train sets off again. When its noise has faded, the man begins to speak:

—You look tired, he says. But you must be able to tell I'm back.

A house stands before him, still and old.

—You are beautiful.

His wrinkled fingers stroke the crumbling walls.

—Look, I open my arms and embrace you, as I embraced the wife I didn't even dream of loving.

A boy appears on the veranda of the house, his eyes turned toward the moon.

The man approaches him.

—I love you, says the man, and he feels that he is speaking those worn-out words for the first time.

The child fixes him with a hard stare.

—Why are you looking at the moon, little boy? asks the man.

—I'm not looking at the moon, the child replies, annoyed. I'm not looking at the moon, I'm looking at the future.

—The future? says the man. That's where I come from. And it's all dead, muddy fields.

—You're lying, you're lying, shouts the child in a rage. There's light there, silver, love, gardens full of flowers!

—That's where I'm from, the man repeats gently, and it's all dead, muddy fields.

Then the child recognizes him and begins to cry. The man feels ashamed.

—But listen, perhaps it's only because I left.

—Really? says the child, reassured. I'm never going to leave.

The woman cried out when she saw the old man sitting on the veranda. At the sound of that cry, he didn't move. But he was not yet dead. He was just sitting there, looking at the sky, and smiling.

## *My Sister Line, My Brother Lanoé*

—My sister Line, I wander the streets, I don't dare tell you, but you know, my sister, my love, your lips, the rims of your ears, my sister Line, for me there are no other girls, only you, my sister Line, I have seen you naked since we were children, without breasts, without sex, it was only your thighs I saw, otherwise you were like me. My sister Line, the years have passed, it is driving me mad to sense your thighs pressed together beside me, your frightened face, your lip trembling with held-back tears. Line, my sister Line. Today in the dirty washing I saw your underpants spotted with blood, you have become a woman, I must sell you, my sister, oh my sister Line!

—My brother Lanoé, is this how it happens? My brother Lanoé, you went out this evening. I stayed here, alone with the old man, and I was afraid because you were gone. Later, they went to bed, the old man and the old woman, but you, brother Lanoé, you hadn't come back. I waited a long time at my window, until you returned with another man. You came into my room, you and the stranger, and I did everything you wanted me to do. I am a woman, brother Lanoé.

I know what I owe the old man and you. I do it willingly, brother Lanoé. I am ready to give my body to anyone. But hold my hand, while the old couple sleeps, stroke my hair, while the other man takes me. Love me, Lanoé, my brother, my love, or tie a rope around my neck.

## *The Mailbox*

I check my mailbox twice a day. At eleven in the morning and five in the evening. Usually the mailman comes before that, in the morning between nine and eleven—it varies a lot; he's very erratic—and in the afternoon around four.

I always go as late as possible, to be sure that he's already passed, otherwise the empty box will give me false hope. I'll think: "Maybe he still hasn't come," and I'll have to go down again, later on.

Have you ever opened an empty mailbox?

Of course. Everyone has. But you couldn't care less. To you, it makes no difference whether it's empty or there's something in there, a letter from your mother-in-law, an invitation to an opening, a card from your friends on vacation.

I don't have a mother-in-law; I'd need to have a wife for that.

I don't have parents, or brothers, or sisters.

Not that I know about, anyway.

I was born in an orphanage. Not actually born there of course, but that's where I became aware of being in the world.

At first it seemed natural to me. That was what I thought life was: lots of children, older or younger, more or less mean, and some adults who were there to protect us from the older ones. I didn't know that in other places there were children who had parents, a father, a mother, sisters, brothers—a family, as they say.

I met them later on, those children from another world, with their parents and brothers and sisters.

And then I began to imagine the parents I must have had—since babies don't grow in cabbage patches—and my siblings, or maybe just one, a brother, or a sister.

I placed my hope in the mailbox.

I waited for a miracle, a letter saying something like: "Jacques, at last I have found you; I am your brother, François."

Naturally, I would have preferred: "Jacques, at last I have found you; I am your sister, Anne-Marie."

But neither François nor Anne-Marie found me.

Nor did I find them.

I would also have been satisfied with a letter from my mother or father. I imagine they're still alive, since I'm fairly young. One or the other might have written to me. For example, my mother:

"Dear Jacques, I hear you have done well for yourself. You've come a long way: congratulations! As for me, I'm still living in misery and poverty, like when you were born. But I'm happy to know you're comfortable at last. It's your father's fault I couldn't keep you and raise you the way I wanted to; he walked out on me when I was pregnant, although I longed to hold you close forever.

"I'm old now, and maybe you could send me some money, seeing as I'm your mother, and in great need on account of my age, because no one will hire me any more. Your mother who loves you and thinks of you often."

Or my father:

"Dear Son, I always hoped I would have a son, and I'm proud of you, because you've done well for yourself. I don't know how you managed it; I've never been successful in anything, although I've worked like a slave my whole life.

"When your mother told me she was pregnant with you, I left on a boat. I lived in ports and bars, and it made me sad to think I had a wife and child somewhere, but I couldn't have you with me, because I earned so little and spent so much of it on drinking to numb the pain I felt inside when I thought of you both. Alcohol and misfortunes have weakened me now, and no one will hire me on the boats any more. I do what I can in the ports, but it's not much. I'm old. So if you could send me some money, given my situation, it would be very welcome. Your loving father, always."

That's the kind of letter I was waiting for, and I would have been so happy to rush to their aid, so delighted to answer their call.

But there was nothing, nothing like that in my mailbox, nothing, until this morning.

This morning I received a letter. It was from one of the city's major entrepreneurs. A very well-known name. I thought it must have been an official letter, a job offer. I'm a decorator. But the letter went like this:

"My son,

"You were just an error of my youth.

"But I assumed my responsibilities. I provided well for your mother; she could have raised you without having to work, but instead she placed you in an orphanage and used my money to go on leading a dissolute life. (I found out she died about ten years ago).

"Because of my public profile, I couldn't intervene directly on your behalf; I already had a legitimate family.

"But I would like you to know that I never forgot you, and all this time, behind the scenes, I have been looking after you. (I was the one who paid your school fees and funded the scholarship for your design course.)

"I have to say that, for your part, you have managed very well, and I congratulate you. You must take after me, because I too started from nothing.

"I don't have any other sons, unfortunately, only daughters, and my sons-in-law are incompetent.

"Now that my life is drawing to a close, I don't care about the conventions. I have decided to entrust you with the management of my business, since I'm weary and I long for rest.

"So I ask you to come and meet me at my office—the address is on the letterhead—on the second of May, at three p.m.

"Your father."

Followed by his signature.

That's the letter I received from my father after thirty years of waiting.

And he is sure that I will go to his office on the second of May, at three p.m., brimming with joy.

The second of May is ten days away.

This evening, I'm sitting in an airport, waiting for a plane to India.

Why India?

Anywhere would do, as long as my "father" can't find me there.

## *Wrong Numbers*

I don't know what it is about my phone number here. It must be similar to a lot of others. I'm not complaining. Every call is a distraction from my dull existence. Since I lost my job, I get a bit bored sometimes. Not always, not really. It's amazing how quickly the days go by. Sometimes I even wonder how we used to fit eight hours of work into a day that's already so short.

The evenings, though, are long and silent. That's why I'm happy when the phone rings. Even if it's usually, almost always, a mistake, and I'm just a wrong number.

People are so scatterbrained.

—Is that the Lanthemann Garage? they ask.

—No, thank you, I say, embarrassed. (I have to get rid of this habit of saying thank you all the time). You've got the wrong number.

—Damn, says the man on the line, my car's broken down on the freeway between Serrières and Areuse.

—I'm sorry, I tell him, I can't repair your car.

—Is that the Lanthemann Garage or what? he says, angry now.

—Excuse me for not being the Lanthemann Garage, but if I can be of help . . .

I always try to be pleasant on the phone, even when it serves no purpose. You never know. Sometimes you make acquaintances, or even friends.

—Yes, you could be of help by bringing me a can of gas.

There's hope in his voice; he thinks he's hit on a sucker, which is true.

—I'm sorry, sir, I don't have any gas, just a little alcohol for a burner.

—Well burn it then, you moron! he says and hangs up.

They're all like that, the wrong numbers. If you don't have what they want right away, they lose interest. We could have had a bit of a chat.

I remember my best ever wrong number. I let the phone ring for a pretty long while. I was going through a very pessimistic phase. It was a woman. At ten o'clock at night.

I put on my languid voice, full of suppressed apprehension.

—Hello?

—Marcel?

—Yes, I say warily.

—Oh, Marcel, I've been trying to find you for ages.

—Likewise.

It's true: I have always been searching for her.

—You too? I knew it. Do you remember, beside the lake?

—No, I don't remember.

I said that because I'm fundamentally honest; I don't like to lie.

—Don't you remember? Were you drunk?

—Possibly, I'm drunk pretty often. Also, my name isn't Marcel.

—Of course not, she retorts. Mine isn't Florence either.

Well, that's something, I know what she isn't called. I'm about to hang up, when she says abruptly:

—It's true, you're not Marcel. But you have a lovely voice.

I don't reply. But she goes on:

—A really pleasant voice, deep and gentle. I would like to see you, meet you.

Still I say nothing.

—Are you still there? Why don't you say something? I know I dialed the wrong number; you're not Marcel, I mean, you're not the man who told me his name was Marcel.

Another silence, especially at my end.

—Are you there? What's your name? Mine is Garance.

—Not Florence? I ask her.

—No, Garance. And yours?

—Mine? Lucien. (It's not, but I don't believe Garance is her real name either.)

—Lucien? That's a beautiful name. Tell me, would you like to meet up?

I say nothing. The sweat is trickling from my forehead down into my eyes.

—It could be fun, says Garance, don't you think?

—I don't know.

—I hope you're not married?

—No, married, no. (Me, married: what a thought!)

—So?

—Yes, I reply.

—Yes, what?

—We could meet up, if you like.

She laughs:

—You're shy, I think. I like shy men. (It must be a change from Marcel.) Listen, here's what I propose. Tomorrow afternoon, between four and five, I'll be at the Café du Théâtre. Tomorrow's Saturday; I'm assuming you don't have to go to work.

She assumes correctly. I don't work on Saturday, or any other day of the week.

—I'll be wearing, she goes on, let's see, a tartan skirt, with a gray blouse and a black cardigan. You'll have no trouble recognizing me. I have dark, midlength hair. Wait. (As if I do anything else.) I'll have a book with a red cover on the table in front of me. And you?

—Me?

—Yes, how will I recognize you? Are you tall, short, thin, fat?

—Me? That's up to you. Medium height, I guess, neither fat nor thin.

—Do you have a mustache or a beard?

—No, nothing. I shave every morning, boringly. (Every three or four mornings, it depends.)

—Do you wear jeans?

—Of course. (I don't, but she must like them.)

—And a big black sweater, I'm guessing.

—Yes, black, usually, I reply to humor her.

—Good, she says, short hair?

—Yes, short, but not cropped.

—Blond or dark?

She's starting to annoy me. My hair's a dirty gray-brown, but I can't admit that.

—Brown, I snap back.

And if she doesn't like it, too bad. Overall I think I preferred the guy with the broken-down car.

—It's all pretty vague, she says, but I'll recognize you. How about you come with a magazine under your arm?

—Which one? (She's pushing it. I never read magazines.)

—Let's say *Le Nouvel Observateur*.

—Yes, I can get *Le Nouvel Observateur*. (Whatever that is, I'll find it.)

—See you tomorrow then, Lucien, she says. And before hanging up, she adds: How exciting!

Exciting! There are people who use that sort of word with ease. I could never talk like that. There are lots of words I'm incapable of saying. For example: "exciting," "thrilling," "poetic," "soul," "suffering," "solitude," and so on. I simply can't bring myself to pronounce them. They make me feel ashamed, as if they were bad words, obscenities, like "shit," "bitch," "pig," "whore."

The next day, I buy a pair of jeans and a big black sweater. The salesman says they really suit me, but I'm not used to clothes like that. I go to the hairdresser too. He offers me a color rinse. I let him do it: dark brown. If it's a failure, I just won't go, too bad. But it's not a failure. Now I have nice brown hair, except I'm not used to it.

I go home and look at myself in the mirror. The hours pass; I keep looking in the mirror. And the other one, the stranger, looks back at me. I don't like him. He's better than I am, more handsome, younger, but he's not me. I wasn't as good, or as handsome, or as young, but I was used to what I was.

Ten to four. Time to go. I change quickly back into my worn brown velvet suit, and I get to the Café du Théâtre at a quarter past four, without having bought a copy of *L'Ancien Observateur*.

I take a seat and look around.

The waiter comes. I order a glass of red wine.

I look around. I see four men playing cards, a bored couple staring into space, and a woman at another table, on her own, wearing a pleated skirt in various shades of gray, a light gray blouse, and a black cardigan. She's also wearing a long necklace made up of three silver chains. (She didn't mention the necklace.) In front of her, a cup of coffee and a book with a red cover.

It's hard to guess her age, because of the distance, but I can tell that she is beautiful, very beautiful, too beautiful for me.

I also see that she has beautiful sad eyes, with a kind of solitude in their depths, and I want to go and speak to her, but I can't bring myself to do it, because I'm wearing my old, worn velvet suit. I go to the restroom and glance in the mirror; I'm ashamed of my brown hair. I'm also ashamed of the impulse that pushed me toward her, toward those "beautiful sad eyes, with a kind of solitude in their depths": it was just a stupid whim of my imagination.

I go back out and choose a new table from which I can observe her at close quarters.

She doesn't look at me. She's waiting for a young man in jeans and a big black sweater, with a magazine under his arm.

She checks the time on the café's clock.

I can't help staring at her, which seems to make her uncomfortable; she calls the waiter and pays for her coffee.

Then the door opens, or rather the leaves of the double door are pushed back, as in a western, and a young man, younger than me, comes in and plants himself in front of the table where Florence-Garance is sitting. He's wearing jeans and a black sweater, and I'm almost surprised not to see the Colt and spurs. He has black, shoulder-length hair, and a handsome beard of the same color. He surveys the customers, including me, and I can hear their conversation clearly.

She says:

—Marcel!

He replies:

—Why didn't you call me?

—Look, I must have got one of the numbers wrong.

—Are you waiting for someone?

—No, no one.

And yet I exist, I'm there, the one she was waiting for, but luckily no one else knows that, and there's no risk of me going over to tell them.

Especially since Marcel says:

—So, shall we go?

—Yes.

She gets up, and off they go.

## *The Countryside*

It was becoming unbearable.

Beneath his windows, which looked over a small, once-charming square, passing cars and revving engines made a din that never stopped.

Not even at night. Impossible to sleep with the windows open.

No, he really couldn't stand it any more.

The children might have been hit by a car as they stepped out of the house. Not a minute of peace.

Miraculously, he was offered a small, secluded farm, abandoned by its owner, going for a song. There was some fixing up to do, of course. The roof, the painting. Putting in a bathroom, too. But even with all that, he was much better off.

And at least the place was his.

He bought milk, eggs, and vegetables from a neighboring farmer for half the price he would have paid in the city supermarkets. And it was pure, natural produce.

The only drawback was the commuting: twelve miles by car, four times a day. But really, twelve miles, that's what? A quarter of an hour.

(Except when there are traffic jams, accidents, a

breakdown, a police check, black ice, or too much snow.)

The school was a bit of a way off too, but a regular half-hour walk is very good for children.

(Except when it's raining, or snowing, too cold or too hot.)

But basically it was paradise.

And he chuckled when he went to the city and parked his car on the little square, often directly beneath what used to be his windows. Breathing the exhaust fumes, he thought with satisfaction of how he had saved his family from all that.

Then there was the road construction project.

Consulting the plans on display at the city hall, he saw that the future six-lane highway would run right through the middle of his farm, or just about. He was deeply shaken, but a moment later he had a sort of illumination: if the route ran through his farm, or his garden, he would be compensated. And he could use that money to buy another farm, somewhere else.

To clarify things, he requested a meeting with the person in charge.

That person greeted him warmly, listened to him politely, and explained that he had misread the plans: the highway in question would be at least five hundred and fifty yards from his farm. So there could be no case for compensation.

The highway was built—a magnificent feat of engineering—and was indeed five hundred and fifty yards away from the farm.

As for the noise, it was barely audible, a sort of continuous hum that you got used to very quickly. And the owner of the farm took comfort from the thought that the new route would reduce his commuting time.

But, as a precautionary measure, he stopped buying milk from his neighbor, because the farmer's cows now grazed beside the highway, where the grass, as everyone knows, contains a lot of lead.

Six months later, gas tanks were installed fifty yards from his farm.

Two years later, an incinerator for household trash, eighty yards away. Heavy trucks came from morning till night, and the chimney smoked continually.

Meanwhile, in the city, cars were banished from the little square. A small garden was established, with flower beds, shrubs, benches to sit on, and a children's playground.

## *The Streets*

From childhood, he had loved walking the streets.

The streets of that town with no future.

He lived in the center, in a narrow, two-story house. The first floor was occupied by his parents' business, a bric-a-brac store full of more or less antique curiosities.

Upstairs, the windows of the cramped apartment looked onto the town's main square, which was deserted by nine at night.

After school, instead of going straight home, he would walk around.

Sitting on a bench or a low wall, he would stare at certain facades.

Since he was a good student, this behavior didn't worry his parents. He was always on time for meals, and in the evenings he played the old out-of-tune piano in his room. It was an item that his parents had never managed to sell, because few people in town could afford a piano, and those who could bought a new one.

He played the old piano every evening.

The rest of the time, he walked around the town. It wasn't a big town, but every day he was able to find a street he'd never seen, or rather hadn't carefully examined.

At first, he contented himself with the old quarter, near his home. The old houses, the castle, the churches, and the crooked streets were enough.

At the age of around twelve, he began to wander farther afield.

He would stop in a village-like street, struck by the houses sunken in the earth and their windows level with the ground.

It was the mood of the streets that attracted him.

An insignificant street could hold his attention for months. He would return in autumn; he wanted to see it again under snow; he wanted to imagine how the houses were furnished and decorated. He took advantage of undrawn curtains and shutters left ajar. He became a voyeur. A voyeur of houses. He had no interest in the people who lived there. Only in the houses and the streets.

The streets!

He wanted to see them in the morning light, and again in the afternoon shadows, when it was raining, and once again when there was fog, or moonlight.

Sometimes he was saddened by the thought that a single life would not suffice for him to know all the streets of his town in their various guises. And he walked until he was worn out, and felt he would never be able to stop.

Then, one day, he had to go away to study music in the capital. He abandoned his old piano and took up the violin. According to his teachers, he was very gifted.

He studied for three years in the Big City.

Three years of nightmares.

Dreams, dreams, every night.

Streets, houses, doors, walls, cobblestones, a sharp pain, waking bathed in sweat in the middle of the night, tuning the violin, not wanting to disturb the others in the house, waiting until he could play at last.

When the day came for him to present his composition to the teacher and the other students, he closed his eyes. The streets of his town filed through the violin, with rests to view an admirable house, or the unforgettable beauty of an empty street.

Solitude rising to a crescendo as he remembered the streets that he had abandoned and betrayed.

Nostalgia and boundless admiration for those beloved streets, a vast sense of guilt, a love at the farthest limit of passion. A stubborn, down-to-earth love, grounded in the earth of that town, a sensual, physical, almost obscene love swept through the music room.

The rebellion of a body that cannot rest anywhere else, of feet that cannot walk anywhere else, of eyes that refuse to see anything else. A soul chained to the walls of that one town, eyes fixed on the facades of that one town.

He knew he would never, ever recover from that mad, unnatural love.

—Quiet! shouted the teacher.

The young man looked up blearily through his tears. He was unaware of what was going on in the room. He didn't care. He lowered his bow.

—What are you all laughing at? asked the teacher.

—Excuse us, sir, said a very gifted student, but it's so schmaltzy.

Finally released from the nightmare, the other students gave their laughter free rein.

The teacher took him to another room.

—Play, he said.

—I can't. Why did they laugh?

—They were embarrassed. They couldn't bear your music . . . your pain. Are you in love?

—I don't understand.

—Feelings aren't really valued in art these days. The fashion's for an almost scientific dryness. And Romanticism, I don't know . . . everything's old hat now, people laugh at everything. Even love. But it's important at your age, it's normal. You're obviously in love with a woman.

Astonished, the student laughed and laughed.

—You need rest, said the teacher. You are a great musician, and from now on, you can work on your own. You can go back home. There's nothing more I can teach you. You have to find your own way. But first, rest.

He went home. To rest from a long absence.

He gave his violin a rest as well. Sometimes he played his old out-of-tune piano. He gave music lessons to earn a living. It suited him very well. He went from student to student, house to house, street to street.

His parents had died. First his father, then his mother. He was no longer sure when.

He walked the streets.

Sometimes he took a newspaper and sat down on a bench. But he didn't read. He took no interest in the news of the world. Nor in the news of his town.

He was just sitting there. He was happy.

For him, the ingredients of happiness were few: wandering the streets, walking the streets, sitting down when he was weary.

Even in his dreams he was walking the streets, and there he was truly happy, because he could walk them all without getting tired, thanks to an unfailing stamina.

One evening, he felt very old, and thought with dread that he would not have time to see a particular house or street again. And it saddened him to think that he would have to return after his death, to walk the streets again and again.

This upset him deeply because he imagined that the children would be afraid of him, and on no account did he want to frighten the children of his town.

He died and, as he had foreseen, he was obliged to return year after year—for eternity—and haunt the streets that he felt he had still not loved enough.

As for the children, he needn't have worried because to them he was just another old man, and to them it made no difference at all whether he was dead or alive.

## *The Big Wheel*

There's someone I've never yet wanted to kill.

It's you.

You can walk in the streets. You can go drinking and walk in the streets. I won't kill you.

Don't be afraid. The city is safe. The only danger in the city is me.

I walk. I walk in the streets. I kill.

But you, you have nothing to fear.

If I follow you, it's because I like the rhythm of your steps. You stagger. It's beautiful. You might be said to limp. And to have a hunchback. Not that you do, really. From time to time, you stand up straight and walk steadily. But I like you late at night, when you're weak, when you stumble, when you stoop.

I'm following you. You tremble. With cold or fear. It's hot, though.

Never, almost never, maybe never has it been so hot in our city.

And what could you be afraid of?

Me?

I'm not your enemy. I love you.

And no one else could harm you.

Don't be afraid. I'm here. I'm protecting you.

And yet I'm suffering too.

My tears—big drops of rain—run down my face. I'm veiled by the night. Lit by the moon. Hidden by clouds. Torn by the wind. I feel a sort of tenderness for you. It comes over me sometimes. Very rarely.

Why for you? I really don't know.

I want to follow you far and wide, wherever you go, for a long time.

I want to see you suffer even more.

I want you to be tired of everything else.

I want you to come and beg me to take you.

I want you to desire me. To want me, love me, call me.

Then I will take you in my arms. I will hold you close. You will be my child, my lover, my love.

I will take you away.

You were afraid of being born, and now you're afraid of dying.

You're afraid of everything.

There's no need to be afraid.

There's just a big wheel turning. It's called Eternity.

I'm the one who turns the big wheel.

You shouldn't be afraid of me.

Or of the big wheel.

The only thing that can scare you and hurt you is life, and you know life already.

## *The Burglar*

Keep your doors shut tight. I come without a sound, wearing black gloves.

I'm not the brutal kind. Or the greedy, stupid kind.

You might admire the delicate pattern of veins on my temples and my wrists, should the occasion arise.

But I don't enter your rooms until late at night, when the last guest has left, and your hideous chandeliers are switched off, and everyone is asleep.

Keep your doors shut tight. I come without a sound, wearing black gloves.

I come for just a few moments, but every night, without fail, to every house, without exception.

I'm not the brutal kind. Or the greedy, stupid kind.

When you wake up in the morning, count your money, your pieces of jewelry: nothing will be missing.

Nothing but a day of your life.

## *The Mother*

Her son left home very young, at eighteen. A few months after the death of his father.

She went on living in the two-bedroom apartment; she was on very good terms with her neighbors. She worked as a cleaner, did mending and ironing.

One day her son knocked at the door. He wasn't alone. There was a girl with him, quite pretty.

She took them in with open arms.

She hadn't seen her son for four years.

After the evening meal, he said:

—Ma, if it's OK with you, we're going to stay here.

Her heart leaped for joy. She prepared the bigger, better bedroom for them. But they went out around ten.

"They must have gone to the movies," she said to herself, and she went to sleep, happy in the little bedroom behind the kitchen.

She was no longer alone. Her son was back living with her.

She left early in the morning to do the cleaning and the odd jobs that she had no wish to give up now, with the change in her situation.

She prepared good lunches for them. Her son always

made a contribution. Flowers, a dessert, wine, or occasionally champagne.

She wasn't bothered by the comings and goings of the strangers she encountered from time to time in the corridor.

—Come in, come in, she would say, the young ones are in their room.

Sometimes, when her son wasn't there, and the two women were sharing a meal, the mother's eyes would meet the sad and dark-ringed eyes of the girl who now lived in her home. And she would look down and mumble, rolling a ball of bread between thumb and fingers:

—He's a good boy. A nice boy.

The girl would fold her napkin—she was polite—and leave the kitchen.

## *Revenge*

He has turned to the right and to the left; he sees nothing.

He is scared. He might even have cried. He's not sure; it might just be the rain on his face.

Above, gray sky; below, mud, the closest thing to him.

He says:

—Why did you disappear? Your glass hands are transparent like the clear water of mountain streams. Silence is written in your eyes, disgust upon your face.

The following day he says:

—Giggling pleasure, your face is black, and yet I would like to reach the white mountain, the one sought by the travelers who lean from the windows of the train without rails, without hope. Travelers without a destination who, when the time comes, hang on the emergency alarms. They swing there, along with my father, while our never-born children weep and bawl between the wheels, at the far end of a path marked out by a million stars.

On the third day, he says:

—Those who were beaten took the blows without

returning them. But they have turned bad. When evening came they crossed the river to wait for the time of reckoning behind the roadblocks.

Even the innocent were slaughtered.

On the last day, with his hair blowing in the wind, he says:

—Don't ask me, don't ask who started it, don't ask who ended it. All I know is there was a first blow.

—I will avenge you.

He lay down beside what had been the body of a woman and caressed her wet hair, or perhaps it was just grass.

Then a hundred men appeared in full view on the field plowed by gunfire and asked:

—When will we be done mourning and avenging our dead? When will we be done killing and mourning? We are the survivors, the cowards, incapable of fighting, incapable of killing. We want to forget. We want to live.

The man in the mud moved, raised his gun, and shot them, every last one.

## *About a City*

It was small and quiet, with squat houses and narrow streets; it had no particular beauty.

I don't know why I talk about it so much, but if I didn't, the shadows of the high, dark mountains around it would smother me.

Sometimes at dusk the sky there took on such extraordinary shades that people would come out of their houses and try to name the colors. But the blends were so strange no name was right for them.

I have spoken of this already, often, and of the house, our house, but I forgot to mention the trees in the garden.

From the start of summer, on one of those trees, we used to find apples that were as sweet as honey, although still unripe. What they tasted like when fully mature is something I never discovered because we always ate them too soon.

This has deprived me of a memory, but how could a child have foreseen that?

It's late. Back there, the nights were still. The drawn curtains didn't even stir. Silence hammered the streets. We were scared, because there was always a bad man in black hiding in the mountains, walking to the city, knocking on the locked and bolted doors.

Before the sun comes up, I have to speak about it all.

The river, the well with its dark wheel, the happy, reassuring summers, sun on our faces at five in the morning, the garden in the churchyard.

Autumn would surprise us in that garden every year with a handful of red leaves falling suddenly from the trees, when we thought there were still plenty of fine days left.

It was amazing how they kept falling, forming a thicker and thicker carpet. We would shuffle through them, barefoot—it was still warm—laughing and starting to feel scared again.

## *The Product*

Mr. B was never home early. But he returned in time for dinner with the rest of the family. And being very fond of his family, especially the children, Mr. B insisted that they all wait for him. During those late meals, the children had a tendency to doze off; they ate little, and whined or sniveled.

When Mr. B was feeling tired, he would ask his wife to put them to bed as soon as possible. Then he would switch on the television and fall asleep in his armchair, snoring quietly. On better days, however, he would propose cards or dominoes, or a board game.

Mr. B's wife would, as a rule, decline this generous offer, and retire to a corner of the room they called the lounge to read a book.

Mr. B had long since resigned himself to the ways of his wife. So he made no remarks about her absence from those educational games which serve to reinforce family bonds. She had no sense of family, or of education. But since she was, after all, the mother of his children, Mr. B overlooked his wife's faults, not without a certain residual resentment.

Mr. B began to come home later and later. The Product was selling poorly, and Mr. B was Sales Manager.

Someone who has never occupied that position cannot possibly imagine the responsibilities that weigh on the shoulders of a Sales Manager. The Product had to be sold, whatever it took.

Conscientious employee that he was, Mr. B did everything he could to sell the Product, and this daily struggle ate into the time that he would have preferred to devote to his family.

When he came home now, long after the evening meal, the children would already be in bed. His wife, reading in a corner of the lounge, would not look up. Mr. B would eat the leftovers—having reheated them himself—and go upstairs to his bedroom, exhausted.

And the Product kept selling less and less, in spite of Mr. B's superhuman efforts.

One night, he was woken by an oppressive sensation. He wanted to speak to his wife. But her bedroom was empty. The wardrobes too. And the drawers. Surprised, he went to the children's bedroom: no one there either.

—It must be the school vacation, he thought. I must have forgotten. I can't keep track of everything.

The next day, at the office, he was notified that he had been laid off.

Permanently. He had been selling the Product badly. A new Sales Manager had just been appointed.

Mr. B went home and waited for the end of the vacation. He looked out the window at the passing clouds. Dust settled everywhere. The dirty dishes piled up in the sink. Mr. B waited, wondering why the school vacation was so long.

## *The Teachers*

During my student years, I had a great affection for my teachers. They filled me with such admiration and respect that I felt obliged to defend them from my classmates' brutality.

The pointless torturing of teachers disgusted me. Even when they gave bad marks. Bad marks are immaterial, so why harm those weak, defenseless creatures?

I remember one of my classmates, a very clever boy, who would sneak up quietly behind our biology teacher, extract the nerves from his spine and hand them out to us.

Quite a few things could be made from those nerves—musical instruments, for instance. The more frayed the nerve, the more delicate the sound.

Our mathematics teacher was very different from the biology teacher. His nerves were no use at all. He did, however, have a completely bald head, on which perfect circles could be drawn with the help of a compass. Circles whose circumferences I noted carefully in my exercise book, to serve as a basis for later deductions.

Naturally, my classmates, the ignorant oafs, found nothing better to do than use my circles as targets for their slingshots—made from the aforementioned nerves—slyly biding their time until the teacher had turned his back to draw the right-angled triangle of Pythagoras's theorem on the blackboard.

Here I would like to add a few words about our talented literature teacher. Just a few, since I know that listeners are soon bored by other people's school-day memories.

On one occasion this teacher threw a piece of chalk at my head to rouse me from my customary morning nap. I detest being woken like that, but I didn't get angry, not at all, so deep was my love for teachers and chalk. I consumed a vast quantity of chalk at the time, because of my calcium deficit. It gave me a slight fever, but I never used that as an excuse to skip school, because—as I keep repeating—I cherished the teaching staff and in particular our (highly talented) literature teacher.

Which is why one day, seized by pity for that unfortunate soul, whose students had just assassinated a poem, at exactly twelve thirty, in the park beside the school, using a skipping rope left behind by the little girls, I put an end to his suffering.

My act of mercy was rewarded with seven years in prison. And yet I've never had cause to regret it, so rich were those seven years in lessons of all sorts, so great my affection for the warders and my admiration for the governor.

But that is another story.

## *I Think*

I have little hope left now. Before, I was searching, I was always on the move. I was waiting for something. For what? I didn't know. But I thought there had to be more to life than that, more than that nothing. Life had to be something, and I was waiting for that something to happen; I was even searching for it.

Now I think there's nothing to wait for, so I stay in my room, sitting on a chair, doing nothing.

I think there is a life outside, but nothing happens in that life. Or not for me.

Maybe things happen for others; it's possible, but that doesn't interest me any more.

Here I am, sitting on a chair, at home. I daydream a bit, but not really. What could I dream of? I'm just sitting here. I can't say I feel good. That's not why I stay here. It's not for the sake of my well-being, on the contrary.

I don't think there's anything good about staying here, and I know I'll have to get up at some point, eventually.

I'm even a bit uneasy about sitting here, doing nothing, for hours on end, or days, I'm not sure. But I can't think of any reason to get up and do something. I simply can't see what I could possibly do.

Obviously, I could tidy up a bit, do some cleaning, all right, there's that.

This place is pretty dirty and messy. I should at least get up and open the window. There's a stale smell of smoke and rot in here.

But I'm not too bothered by any of that. A bit, but not enough to get up. I'm used to the smell. I don't notice it. I just think that if someone happened to come in ... except there is no "someone." Nobody comes in here.

For something to do, I start reading the newspaper that's been lying on the table since ... since I bought it, a while back ...

I don't bother picking it up, of course. I leave it there, on the table, and read it from a distance, but my head or my eyes won't take it in; all I can see are dead black flies, so I stop trying.

Anyway, I know that on the other page, there's a young man, not all that young, my age, sitting in a round, built-in bathtub, reading the same newspaper, looking at the advertisements and the stock prices, completely at ease, a glass of fine whisky within reach on the rim of the tub. He looks handsome, alert, intelligent, well informed.

The mere thought of that image makes me stand up and go and vomit in the sink that isn't built in but just hangs off the wall of the kitchen. And all the stuff that comes out of me blocks up that miserable sink.

I'm truly amazed by the volume of the filth, twice

as much as I could have eaten in the last twenty-four hours, it seems to me. Contemplating the foul mess, I'm overcome by a new wave of nausea, and I rush out of the kitchen.

I go out into the street to clear my head. I walk like everybody else, but there's nothing in the streets, just people, stores, that's all.

I don't want to go back home because of the blocked sink, but I don't want to keep walking either, so I stop on the sidewalk, in front of a department store, facing the street, watching people go in and come out, and I think that those who are coming out should stay in there, and those who are going in should stay out here—that way they could spare themselves a whole lot of movement and fatigue.

It would be good advice, but they wouldn't listen. So I say nothing. I don't move. I'm not even cold here at the entrance, taking advantage of the warmth coming out through the constantly opening doors, and I feel almost as good as before, sitting in my room.

## *My Father*

You never met him.

He's dead.

That's why, at the beginning of December last year, I went back to my country, where you've never been.

A twenty-four hour train trip to the capital, a night of rest at my brother's place, then twelve more hours on the train, that makes thirty-six hours of traveling to that big industrial city where my father was going to be put in a wall: a white porcelain urn, a little hollow in the cement.

Thirty-six hours of train travel, with stops in cold, deserted stations, waiting among fellow travelers who hadn't lost their fathers, or so long ago that they weren't thinking about it. I was thinking about it, but I couldn't believe it was true.

I had done that trip several times already, when my father was still alive. He had waited for me there at the end of the journey, in the suburbs of that industrial city where he had lived and loved so little, where he had never walked with me, hand in hand.

At his funeral, it was almost raining. There were

quite a lot of people, wreaths, songs, a choir of men in black. It was a socialist funeral, without a priest.

I placed a bunch of carnations beside the small white urn, so small I couldn't believe it contained my father, who'd been so big in the days when I was still his daughter, his child.

It wasn't my father, that porcelain urn.

Still, I cried when they put it in the cement wall. From a record player came the national anthem, asking God to bless this land and its people who had suffered so much for the sins of the past and even for those of the future. The choir had to start up again because the two men in charge of sealing the niche were making a mess of it: the plaque wouldn't fasten; the urn, my father, didn't want to go into that little hole in the cement.

Later I learned that he had wanted to be buried, not put in a wall, in the village where he had been born, but as he lay dying from stomach cancer, fading away without knowing what was wrong, his pain relieved by morphine injections, he had been convinced by my mother and brother that he would be better off there, in the cemetery of that horrible industrial city, a city he had never liked, where he had never walked with me, hand in hand.

Afterwards, I had to greet a lot of people I didn't know, but they knew me. The women took me in their arms.

Finally, it was over. Numb with cold, we could go back to my parents' place, my mother's place, I mean. There was a sort of reception. I ate, like everyone else;

I drank. I was tired from the trip, the ceremony, the guests, everything.

I went to my father's little room, where he used to go to read, study languages, and write his diary.

He wasn't there. He wasn't in the garden either. I thought maybe he'd gone out shopping to make sure all the guests were well supplied. He often went shopping, he loved that.

I was waiting for him. I wanted to see him again, because I had to come back soon, back here, that is. I drank a lot of wine, and he still wasn't there.

"But where's Dad got to?" I finally said, and the people looked at me.

My other brothers took me to their place and put me to bed. The next day I left. Twenty-four hours, thirty-six hours of trains.

During the trip, I made plans.

After a while I would come back, I would remove the cement plaque, I would steal the urn, and bury it in the village where he was born, beside the river, in the black earth.

Except I don't know that region. I've never been there. So, having stolen the urn, where would I bury it?

There is no place where my father walked with me, hand in hand.